ARIADNE,
Awake!

Doris Orgel

ARIADNE, Awake!

Illustrated by Barry Moser

VIKING

*I want to thank the following for their help and encouragement:
my agent, Amy Berkower; my editor, Regina Hayes;
Professor Mary Lefkowitz of Greek and Latin Studies at Wellesley College;
Dr. Claudia Lewis, Distinguished Specialist in Children's Literature
at Bank Street College; my friend and colleague Doreen Rappaport;
my friend Dr. Austin Silber; and, not least,
my husband, Dr. Shelley Orgel for valiantly driving us through Sicily,
and for living through this story with me.*

The illustrations for *Ariadne, Awake!* were painted in a traditional transparent watercolor
technique, using British and French pigments. In this technique, known as "paper telling,"
the white of the paper serves as a highlight, and no white pigment is used in the palette.

The watercolor paper was handmade in England by Mr. Simon Green
of the Barcham-Green paper mills in Maidstone, Kent, Great Britain.

The calligraphy was hand lettered by Kate Kiesler.

VIKING
Published by the Penguin Group
Penguin Books USA Inc., 375 Hudson Street, New York, New York 10014, U.S.A.
Penguin Books Ltd, 27 Wrights Lane, London W8 5TZ, England
Penguin Books Australia Ltd, Ringwood, Victoria, Australia
Penguin Books Canada Ltd, 10 Alcorn Avenue, Toronto, Ontario, Canada M4V 3B2
Penguin Books (N.Z.) Ltd, 182–190 Wairau Road, Auckland 10, New Zealand

Penguin Books Ltd, Registered Offices: Harmondsworth, Middlesex, England

First published in 1994 by Viking, a division of Penguin Books USA Inc.

1   3   5   7   9   10   8   6   4   2

Text copyright © Doris Orgel, 1994
Illustrations copyright © Barry Moser, 1994
All rights reserved

Library of Congress Cataloging-in-Publication Data
Orgel, Doris. Ariadne, awake! / Doris Orgel ; illustrated by Barry Moser.   p.   cm.
Summary: Fourteen-year-old Ariadne, princess of Crete, helps her beloved
Theseus escape death in the labyrinth of the monstrous Minotaur.
ISBN 0-670-85158-2
1. Ariadne (Greek mythology)—Juvenile fiction.   2. Theseus (Greek mythology)—
Juvenile fiction.   [1. Ariadne (Greek mythology)—Fiction.   2. Theseus
(Greek mythology)—Fiction.]   I. Moser, Barry, ill.   II. Title.
PZ7.O632Ar   1994   [Fic]—dc20   93-24123   CIP   AC

Printed in Singapore   Set in 12 point Sabon
Without limiting the rights under copyright reserved above, no part of this publication may be
reproduced, stored in or introduced into a retrieval system. or transmitted, in any form or by any
means (electronic, mechanical, photocopying, recording or otherwise), without the prior written
permission of both the copyright owner and the above publisher of this book.

In memory of my mother,
Erna Adelberg
—D. O.

For my friend, Willa Perlman,
with great affection
—B. M.

Prologue

LONG AGO, IN ANCIENT CRETE, King Minos pledged to sacrifice a splendid white bull to the god Poseidon. But he failed to keep his word. He sacrificed an ordinary bull to the god instead of the splendid one.

Poseidon took revenge. He caused King Minos's queen, Pasiphae, to be seized by a passion for the splendid white bull that was to have been sacrificed to him.

At that time the famous inventor and artisan Daedalus lived and worked in Crete. Queen Pasiphae begged him to help her.

Daedalus constructed a beautiful cow which was hollow inside. The queen could lie down inside the cow. In this way she could come together with her beloved.

To King Minos's rage and shame, the queen conceived. In due time she gave birth to a creature with a human body and the head of a bull. They named him Minotaur.

Daedalus then built a maze known as the Labyrinth. There they kept the Minotaur. And no one was allowed to enter except his keepers, and fourteen luckless young Athenians whom he devoured yearly.

USIC SANG
in my dream. Radiance glowed and shimmered. My lion's eyes lit
up with it, as though he were springing to life. The radiance grew.
A stranger appeared. In his hand he held whatever it was that shone
so bright—a ring? A cluster of gems? I was dazzled. I could not
see. I sensed a great danger about to engulf me. And yet, in dreams'
mysterious way, bliss awoke inside me, happiness I had not known
since my mother died.

The music changed to roaring. I thought, while still half asleep,
"It's my lion leaping from the painting on my wall." No. The roaring
came from far away and from deep below.

I opened my eyes. Then I knew: It came from the prison maze at
the westernmost end of the palace.

It was the Minotaur. A cruel monster—yes. How could he not
be cruel, locked away from kindness? He hungered for human
flesh—yes, of course. How could he not, when that was all his
keepers fed him?

I wanted to see him. It was my right. More than my right. I felt
it was my duty; he was my kin.

I got up and went over to Cleia. She slept on a cot in an alcove of my bedroom. My thirteen other serving women slept in communal quarters outside the royal apartments.

Cleia was the youngest, yet more skilled in serving me than all the others put together. She could brush the knots and tangles from my thick, wild hair without pulling and hurting, and make rows of ringlets across my forehead that looked almost natural. She knew exactly what mixture of fragrances to pour into my baths, and which tunic or gown, sandals, cinch belt, and jewels I would want to wear.

My father had given her to me five years before, along with the stern warning: "It is undignified and pathetic when princesses make friends of slaves. Do not grow fond of her."

I disobeyed right from the start. Soon she shared in all my moods. I tried to share in hers. We laughed and played together when we were merry, and wept and comforted each other when we were sad.

"Cleia, listen." I bent over her, touched her shoulder. "Wake up! Come with me!"

She shuddered, as though she, too, had heard the roaring, and said, "No."

"Come on, Cleia. We'll be quiet as mice. Don't be afraid."

"Yes, I am. You should be, too. The M—" She dared not say his name. "The monster would eat us alive!"

"Not so, I promise you. He will know me, I feel certain. Yes, he must. We are kin. He is my brother—"

"No!" She could not bear to think it. She put her hand over my mouth.

I pushed it away. "My half brother, then. Son of my mother, whom I loved. I miss her with every breath."

Cleia stroked my cheek. "Yes, I know." She, too, had lost her mother when she was taken into slavery. "But giving birth to the M—the monster is what killed your mother."

"Yes, but that was not his fault. Listen. Do you hear how mournful he sounds? He has never had comforting. Perhaps that is what he needs."

Cleia held me to her, as though I were still little. "Go back to bed," she said, stroking my hair.

"Don't tell me what to do, Cleia. Bring me my shawl. And my bracelets."

She brought me the wrong ones.

"Not those. *You* know which ones."

I wanted my snake bracelets, given to me by the high priestess of Mother Dia of the Earth.

"Ariadne, you know well that you may only wear those bracelets on occasions sacred to the Goddess," said Cleia as though she were my teacher.

"As future high priestess to the Goddess, I know what I know and must do as I must," I answered, and went to get the bracelets myself.

Cleia tried to bar my way. She was twelve, two years older than I. But I was stronger. I pushed past her, opened the oakwood chest that held my jewels, took out the sacred bracelets, put them on. The snakes, pieced together of onyx, emeralds, ivory, and rose quartz, coiled around my wrists, spiraled up my arms like living creatures, eyes gleaming as though they could see, fangs sharp as though ready to sink into flesh.

I took out my magic key as well.

Then, on a whim, I snatched a handful of mimosa blooms from a vase by my bed.

"Blossoms? For the monster?" Cleia laughed at me. But she also wept that she could not prevent me. "Wait. The night is cold." She brought me her own shawl and placed it about my shoulders.

"Thanks." I put my arms around her. An awful sadness seized me that I could not name.

I shook it off. And I ran, barefoot for silence and secrecy's sake, out my door, down the long corridor past the royal apartments, to the pillared marble staircase, down five flights to the level that lay below ground.

Our palace was a city unto itself. As many people lived in it as in all the rest of Knossos.

Below ground were storage rooms, armories, stables, shut up for the night. All was quiet. One time I heard footsteps and squeezed into a doorway, not breathing till they passed.

I ran for as long as I had breath. Finally I came to the westernmost portal. It was black and unadorned. Crete's sacred double-bladed ax, the *Labrys,* was mounted on it. Three iron locks locked it tight.

I took my key, which Daedalus had given me. It was bronze, quite ordinary looking. But it could open any lock, so Daedalus had promised.

And so it did, all three. The portal sprang open wide.

I could not see beyond the first dark, walled-in passageway of the dreaded Labyrinth. But I knew, all Crete knew, of its vastness. It covered more ground than all our spacious royal pleasure gardens and all the other gardens inside the confines of the palace. "It has thousands of twists and treacheries," my old nurse used to say. "It has more turnings than bulls' hides have hairs, but there's no returning, of that you may be sure."

Oh, but for me there would be a returning. Not in vain was I the Minotaur's half sister. Not in vain did I have the world-famous inventor Daedalus for my teacher. If need be, I, too, could invent things—at least so I thought.

Cleia's shawl was loosely woven. I pulled two threads out—one blue, one red—planning to make a knot in the blue thread every time I turned left, and a knot in the red thread every time I turned right. Then, later, those knots would guide me out. I congratulated myself on how simple it seemed. And I entered.

The first passageway was open to the sky. Moonlight shone in. Vines and creepers climbed the stone walls so that it looked almost gardenlike.

The roaring had stopped. When I came to the first turning place, I heard it again. I used it as my guide.

It grew louder with every turn I made.

At the tenth turn I saw something white on the ground. It was a bone. I'd often seen sheep and cattle bones on the altars of our gods. But this one was a human bone, gnawed clean.

Again the roaring stopped. All was eerily still. I ran my fingers up my bracelets, touching the jeweled snakes' backs. I prayed to the goddess whose creatures they were: "Great Mother Dia, tell me which turn to take."

Then I felt a shaking. Was it my own trembling? Yes. But it was also like when Earthshaker Poseidon was angry and shook the ground. Had I roused that god's anger by coming to this place? Would he now punish me?

The ground shook more.

Next instant, from around the turning, appeared two sharp-tipped horns. Then I beheld the giant head—of a bull. His eyes were bloodshot, his nostrils afoam. Spittle hung from his muzzle.

From his bull's neck down, he had a human body, far bigger and stronger than that of a full-grown man—even though, counting by human time, only five years had gone by since his birth. Enormous muscles rippled in his arms, chest, thighs. A bull's tail swung behind him.

He lowered his great head and came rushing straight toward me. A horrible sound came from his throat. He was entirely bestial. He could no more sense that I was his kin and had come to comfort him than he could have sung me a poem or plucked a tune on a harp.

I dropped the shawl, the mimosa blooms. "Mother, you died of this Minotaur," I thought, or perhaps I breathed the words aloud. "Be with me now, as I, too, must die."

His left horn shot forward, pointing at my throat.

I held out my snake bracelets, in vain.

So then I prayed to Hermes. When humans die, he carries their souls away. "Swift, gentle god, I thank you." For I felt no pain, only everything around me growing dark.

When I regained consciousness, a keeper had me in his arms.

"Don't betray me," I begged. "If you honor the Mother Goddess in whose name I am to rule, swear you won't."

"Princess most pure, I won't." Then he warned me, "Don't look back."

But I did.

I saw a young girl in my place. She wore a fillet in her hair, Athenian style. Her hands and feet were shackled. The Minotaur sank his horns into her belly. It ripped open. Blood spurted out.

Then everything went dark, black all around as in death's kingdom.

Chapter 2

I AWOKE IN MY OWN BED with Cleia's shawl around me. For a moment I felt safe. Then, touching my wrists, I was filled with foreboding. One snake bracelet was missing.

I looked in my jewelry chest. The bracelet was not there.

"Cleia, Cleia!" I shouted. No reply.

My old nurse and three others of my women came in. "Where is Cleia?" I asked. They shook their heads and would not say.

I asked them to look for my bracelet. They could not find it anywhere.

When they dressed me, a servant of my father's burst in. Without knocking. Without so much as "beg your pardon," or "by your leave," he said that I was to go to the throne room. He had orders to take me there "at once."

It was the place where grand receptions were held. My father had sometimes invited me there to dance before ambassadors and other honored guests. I persuaded myself this was the reason he wanted me there now, though it seemed an unusual hour.

"Wait outside," I told my father's servant.

I changed from the heavier tunic the women had chosen into a short, saffron-colored *chiton* of airy linen. I put on my softest, lightest sandals. Yes, I would dance. Dancing would free me from the night's terror that still clung to me.

I looked in the mirror. My cheeks were pale. I pinched them a little. I was ready.

My old nurse wanted to accompany me, but I did not let her. I ordered my father's servant to follow me at a respectful distance. I went to the throne room as though of my own accord, head high, but with dread and foreboding.

Instead of distinguished visitors from foreign places, children sat in the richly upholstered seats, the daughters and sons of all the nobles, merchants, soldiers, guards, grooms, and officials who lived within the palace.

My father sat towering on his throne of snow-white marble. He wore a royal blue, bejeweled robe and his high, jewel-studded crown with peacock feathers sweeping down, as he did on occasions of great pomp and ceremony.

Seven bodyguards attended him—and one other. This other wore the white kilt and helmet that only the Minotaur's keepers wore.

He was the keeper who had rescued me.

He stared at the floor, avoiding my gaze.

In my mind's eye I heard him saying, "Princess most pure, I won't."

But yes, he *had* betrayed me—had taken the bracelet from my arm and shown it to my father as proof of where I'd been.

"Ariadne, approach," said my father.

I came forward. So did the keeper, and handed me back the bracelet. I did not want to put it on. It was desecrated. The snake looked lifeless. Its eyes were dull, unseeing.

My father touched his scepter to the keeper's shoulders. "I hereby name you captain of the keepers." He gave him a purse of money for thanks. Then he called, "Bodyguards' captain, step forward."

The bodyguards' captain came toward me brandishing the whip he had been holding behind his back.

I looked my father in the eyes. They were as cold as if he had never held me or dandled me on his knee when I was small.

He raised his scepter high. "Children of the palace, watch carefully. Be warned. Recall to your memories what you are about to witness, if ever you are tempted to enter forbidden places and do forbidden deeds as this princess has done." He pointed the scepter in my direction. "Ariadne, kneel."

Ariadne means "most pure, most sacred." And so I was—and am. I remained standing, straight as a column, and swore this silent, solemn oath: "I shall not kneel to anyone but Mother Dia, Great Goddess of the Earth, whose high priestess I will be when I assume the crown."

"Ariadne, did you not hear me?" shouted my father. "I ordered you to kneel!"

He gave a signal and the bodyguards' captain pushed me down. He swung the whip behind his back. It sang in the air.

"Great Goddess, tear the whip to shreds. Let it not touch me," I prayed.

Goddesses and gods take action or not, when and as they choose. The whip came down on my back five times, stinging my flesh, drawing blood. But the pain of it was mild, compared to a new feeling that was taking root in me—a sharp and bitter hatred for my father.

Later, I learned my further punishment: He had taken Cleia away from me. I never saw her again.

Chapter 3

CRETE WAS A POWERFUL KINGDOM. Our forests gave us timber for building mighty ships. Our warships rid the sea of pirates, made it safe for our merchant ships to do trade near and far. Other, lesser kingdoms grew to fear us and agreed to my father's demand that they pay us tribute—shipments each year of metals, spices, ivory, and such.

Athens, then weak and small, was our foe. My father made its citizens pay the costliest tribute—human flesh. Every spring, in the month when mimosa trees came into bloom, a ship with a black sail arrived in our harbor with fourteen young Athenians aboard.

Beginning when I was ten, the year I had ventured into the Labyrinth, my father insisted I go with him to "greet" the victims. By this he meant looking them over, making sure that Athens was not cheating us by sending any who were sickly, weak, or maimed.

I watched as our officials went aboard and led the victims off the ship. But then I always turned away. I could not bear to look for long at the terror on their faces.

My father laughed at me for that. He unashamedly enjoyed seeing others suffer. "It's a healthy sight," he said. "It makes you glad that

13

you are who you are. Go on, look them in the eyes. Pity is a weakness. Rip it from your heart."

I had seen four black-sailed ships arrive, counted four times fourteen young Athenians, fifty-six in all, landing on our shore to meet their death.

Now, on a sunny, windswept morning, the fifth ship lay at anchor in the harbor. It was longer and narrower, built for greater speed than the others. Its bow was in the shape of a bird's beak. Written on the side was the name SEA DOVE.

Our harbor officials had already gone aboard with prison garb for the victims: coarsely woven, blood-red tunics. "Loosen their ankle chains," ordered my father. "Let the victims disembark."

The youngest—a boy, perhaps eleven, a girl no older than ten— were first to cross the plank. Tears streamed down their cheeks, and they could not even wipe them away, for their hands were bound behind their backs.

The older ones were stauncher, did not allow themselves to cry. I noticed that many kept turning their heads, looking to someone behind them.

This time I forced myself to look into their faces and I did not turn away. I searched my inmost feelings to test what my father had said. When I saw a boy stumble and an official jab him in the side, it caused me pain. I found no shred of pleasure in comparing these victims' suffering to my own good fortune. And I promised myself that when I ascended the throne of Crete, my first action would be to end this cruelty.

The-next-to last victim was a well-formed, bright-haired young woman walking alone. My father smacked his lips in crude appreciation of her beauty.

She heard. She turned around to the young man who came last to see if he had heard it, too.

This young man moved with a grace and suppleness his shackles could not diminish. A purple cloak hung from his shoulders. His hair was twisted into a warrior's knot and shone like summer wheat. His lips were full, his nose was straight and fine. His eyes were the color of sunlight on the sea. He looked as little like a victim as the noonday sun looks like a sputtering candle flame.

Seeing him drove all else from my mind except the wish that he look at me.

"You with the cloak, approach!" shouted my father. "Don't I know you? You are the king's son, are you not? What are you doing here?"

The young man answered, "I am he."

"You cast your lot with commoners? You must be mad. Did no one tell you that princes are exempt?"

"The kind of king I hope to be is not exempt from his subjects' fate," replied this prince.

"Nobly reasoned," said my father. "Except you'll never be that kind, or any other kind of king, just a heap of bones picked clean. I've forgotten your name. What is it?"

"Theseus, son of King Aegeus. Although some say that—" Theseus cast down his eyes.

"That what? Out with it!"

"That Poseidon, god of earthquakes and the sea, was present at my making."

"Poseidon's son, are you? Beware. The gods punish braggarts." My father gave a loud guffaw.

"They also punish those who speak their names without awe," said Theseus quietly. "I am not a braggart. This much I know: The sea god holds me dear and has often helped me."

"Has he? Let us see if he will help you now." My father shouted to a guard, "Remove this victim's chains."

15

The guard did so.

My father turned, strode down the path that led to the end of the harbor. "Theseus, follow me!"

Theseus stood still. What I had wished now happened: He turned his eyes on me. It only lasted a moment. But when it ended I felt changed, as though my childhood had slipped from me like an outworn garment, and I had come into womanhood.

"Very well, Minos, I follow," called Theseus. I followed, too, stride for stride. I could not have done otherwise. It seemed to me as though the whole wide earth held no other place for me than close by Theseus's side.

The harbor path led to a jetty. The jetty stretched far into the sea. At the end of it loomed three dark, jagged rocks.

My father, though advanced in years, climbed the outermost rock with much agility. "Theseus, come up here!"

When they reached the top, my father took off his signet ring. He showed it to Theseus, then with a mighty swing of his arm, hurled it far into the waves. "Fetch back my ring for me, and may Poseidon help you."

My father laughed, but quickly stopped. For suddenly the sea turned fierce and roiling. A storm arose with waves as high as walls.

Theseus stripped off his clothing. He stood poised for an instant, arms arching forward. Then he swooped into the air, gliding, soaring, and plunged into the white crested waves like a sea eagle after its prey.

During the endless time that he stayed under, I, too, could not draw breath. Not till his head resurfaced did I gasp and fill my lungs. The storm still raged, the sky was dark. But for me, seeing Theseus safe restored the world to brightness.

He rode the wild waves as though they were obedient horses. He leaped onto the jetty. "Here is your ring, Minos." He gave it back.

In his other hand he held an object so dazzling that it blinded me. I had to shut my eyes. When I opened them again I saw what it was: a golden band, such as brides wear on their heads, exquisitely wrought, studded with brilliant gems.

"Princess most beautiful, this is for you," he said.

I bowed my head. I felt as though in a dream.

I'd often been told I was beautiful and taken it for mere politeness, flattery. I had mirrors that showed me clearly my distinctions and my flaws.

But when Theseus crowned me with this incomparable band and I looked into his eyes, his eyes were my mirrors, and I saw it was true. Yes, I was beautiful.

"Amphitrite sends you this gift," said Theseus.

"Poseidon's wife? Queen of the deep?" my father scoffed. "More likely you bought it cheap from some Athenian trinket monger. Let me see." He reached for the band.

I held on to it with all my strength.

"Minos, leave off," Theseus warned.

My father persisted, trying to pry my fingers loose.

Theseus leaned forward, made a summoning motion to the sea. At once a giant wave rose up, taller than a ship's mast.

We dropped to our knees, clung to the edge of the jetty. A mountain of water crashed over us.

I thought I had drawn my last breath, and yet I felt happy as never before. For Theseus was by my side, holding me safe. This seemed worth the whole rest of my life to me. The sea water was icy cold, yet I felt warm through and through. My body, my whole self rejoiced in his touch.

As fast as it had risen up, the wave retreated. We were safe, breathing air again. I felt for the golden band. It still encircled my brow.

My father was chastened. He made no further attempt to take it from me.

We started back toward the harbor. Litter bearers and others of our retinue came rushing to our aid.

A guard asked if Theseus was to be put back in shackles.

"No." My father gave orders that he be treated with respect and courtesy.

He rode with us in our litter. When we passed the prison house that stood close by the harbor, my father said, "Your fellow Athenians will be confined in there. But you shall stay in the palace. Tomorrow night we hold a feast in honor of your ship's arrival. Will you do us the honor of attending?"

"I will, with pleasure," Theseus replied.

"Good. You shall enjoy yourself while you can. I will give orders that you be the last to go into the Labyrinth. That way you will have more time."

"No, Minos. As prince, I must go first."

"Just as you wish. Then you'd better enjoy yourself all the more, for tomorrow will be your last day alive. You shall enter the Labyrinth at sunrise, the day after tomorrow." My father shrugged his shoulders. "I only hope your princely blood won't spoil the Minotaur's appetite for that of commoners."

Then a courier ran up with a message. While my father leaned out the window to receive it, I whispered, "Theseus, change your mind. Go last."

"I can't. But don't worry. Last and first will be the same."

"What do you mean? I don't understand."

"You will," he said with perfect calm.

Chapter 4

ON THE DAY BEFORE THE FIRST victim entered the Labyrinth, it was the custom to make offerings to Zeus, Hera, and Poseidon and ask them to sanction the occasion.

No offerings were made to Mother Dia on this day. On the contrary, her priestess shunned her sacred places. For it was feared that the Goddess of the Earth looked unfavorably on blood sacrifices.

Aphrodite also received no offerings on this day. Yet, when I awoke I felt her calling me to come to her.

It was early. My women were still in their quarters. I dressed myself and hurried to the easternmost palace gate.

This led to a hillside sloping seaward, covered with red valerian in full bloom and sky-blue myrtle blossoms. I picked as many myrtle blossoms as my arms could hold, for they were Aphrodite's favorites.

At the bottom of the hill stood a shrine to her. Whenever a great wave crashed to shore it left a lacework of foamy spray along the base of the altar.

"Mighty goddess, into whose power I have come, accept these offerings," I prayed, heaping myrtle around the statue's feet.

A breeze started up. An apple tree, sacred to her, clung to the sloping soil just above the shrine. The breeze stirred in its branches. Apple blossom petals wafted down. They settled in my hair and on the golden band.

I took it as a sign of Aphrodite's favor. I beseeched her, "Goddess, stand by Theseus—"

"She does," said he, confident and laughing, scrambling down the slope. "With those blossoms in your hair, you look like a bride."

He bowed to the statue. But he called her "Epitragia." I had not heard that name before.

We found a rock with a hollowed-out place, sat there together overlooking the sea. And he told me a strange story:

"When I was still in Athens, I asked Aphrodite if I was doing right to come here, and if she would champion my journey. I offered up a goat to her, a milk-white she-goat. Then a wonderful thing happened. Even as the priestess lowered the knife, the goat turned male. I would not have believed it, except I saw it with my own eyes. It was Aphrodite's doing. That is why in Athens we now call her Epitragia, changer of goats. It was her way of answering yes, she would champion my journey to Crete, where"—Theseus paused and looked deep into my eyes—"I found you, my Ariadne." His finger moved across my cheek and sent ripples of joy all through me.

He took a petal from my hair, put it to his lips. "Apple blossoms in your hair and on your golden headband do indeed make you look like a bride." He took my face in both his hands and said, "Aphrodite approves. She will champion us both."

"Us"—the word seemed wholly new. It began a song that sang and sang in me as I stayed in his arms, I don't know how long.

The sun's heat burning down restored me to reason. "It's getting late," I said. "You must hurry back to the palace, or people will wonder where you are."

"Yes, you are right. First, though, come with me."

We went to the shrine and embraced before the statue, holding each other close. "This, too, is prayer," murmured Theseus, "the kind Aphrodite understands best."

Then he grasped the apple tree's sturdiest branch and swung on it. More blossom petals showered down. "The goddess smiles on us," he called, and ran up the slope.

Perhaps she did. But Zeus did not. And his priests were impatient with me, for I arrived late at his altar and had kept them waiting.

The chief priest handed me the sacred pitcher. I waited till the smoke from the burning thighbones and fat of sheep had risen beyond the treetops. Then I poured out the libation onto the altar and began the prayer: "Skyfather Zeus, accept these gifts, and keep us free of . . ." I faltered. I had not forgotten the words, it was just that they were hard to say: ". . . keep us free of guilt and blame for the Athenian blood that must be spilled tomorrow."

Must? A clamor started in my mind. "Must *not* be spilled tomorrow!" I almost cried aloud.

Chapter 5

A HUNDRED AND FIFTY GUESTS ATTENDED the feast. Thirty servants waited on them, offering fresh baked bread, olives, dainty greens, and succulent meats that had been roasting over open fires all day. Twenty more servants filled guests' drinking bowls with honey-sweetened ale.

Twelve musicians tuned their harps and lyres, readied their pipes and flutes.

When I was small, on banquet nights, I would lie in my bed listening hard, trying to hear the music, imagining the splendor, wishing away the years till I could be there. Now here I was, at the very head of it, but I had no appetite for food or drink, for witty talk or laughter. My one desire was to be with Theseus.

He was far down the hall where the lesser guests reclined.

I had to grip the scrollwork of my couch arms to keep from leaping up and going to him. This would have been a serious breach of manners and thrown my father into a rage.

Not that my father's manners were all that fine. He chewed ravenously on a lamb shank and washed it down with noisy gulping. Fatty juice dripped down his chin and stained his robe. Between taking bites and gulps he turned his attention to a gaudily painted woman who knelt beside his couch, and caressed her in a manner I could not abide.

I faced the other way. From this position I looked straight into the furious eyes of giant blood-red bulls with gold-tipped horns painted in all too lifelike fashion on the wall.

Such a fear took hold of me, it would have caused me to grow numb if I had stayed still one second longer. I stood up and made my way to the left side of the hall toward the musicians.

Below the musicians' platform was our wonderful mosaic. Its fame had spread to distant places. Visitors came from abroad just to admire it. Its highly polished stone chips were of rich and subtle colors. Its design, which Daedalus had drawn, consisted of myriad lines, shapes, angles, somehow magically pleasing to the eye, though they told no story, held no meaning—or so it seemed to those who did not know its secret.

"Play something never heard before," I said to the musicians' leader.

He was startled. "You mean, compose a new air, here and now?"

"Yes. Invite your muses. Trust them to inspire you."

I pressed three fingers of both hands to both sides of my head, calling to Terpsichore, my muse, to come to me.

She did. She inspired me with dances never danced before. She took hold of passions in me, formed them into patterned motions that my feet and my entire body made, gliding, swooping, whirling.

I danced the radiance of Theseus's arrival. I danced the bloodthirst and cruelty of the man-beast Minotaur. I danced my rage, my shouts of "No!" to fears of Theseus succumbing. I danced my will that Theseus live and flourish in the fullness of my love.

He felt it. It drew him. He leaped up from his couch and came striding toward me.

26

Threatening looks and gestures assailed him from all sides.

"Stop!" called my father, to no avail. Then he forgot the lesson of the giant wave washing over the jetty and shouted, "Theseus, you insult our hospitality. Guards, remove him!"

Five guards ran to obey. Theseus pummeled them with his fists, pushed them to the floor. The floor heaved up—from those guards' weight, I thought at first. Then came thunder crashing and roaring. Couches and tables slid forward. Platters, goblets, bowls upended, clattered down. I clutched the railing of the musicians' platform, trying to stay upright. But I fell. Everything, everybody, fell.

Only Theseus remained standing. His feet were planted solid as two mighty trees on the heaving ground. Once again Poseidon had come to his aid.

When the quaking eased, the guards crept around on all fours, making pitiful attempts to grasp hold of Theseus.

My father had relearned the lesson. He commanded, "Let him be." And he prayed, "Earthshaker god, Poseidon, pardon."

Poseidon must have heard him. The quaking stopped.

Theseus and I, as though the same thought guided us, moved onto the mosaic floor with our arms extended to each other. Whichever deities inspired us inspired the musicians also. They took up their instruments, resumed playing.

In all the thousands of years there had been dancing in this palace, always only women danced with women, men with men. Never in Knossos, or anywhere in Crete, had a woman and a man joined together in a dance.

Now it happened.

Theseus and I danced as though we were one.

The music became ever more melodious, ever more filled with delight. It was as though the muse Euterpe herself had joined in and were playing her double flute.

All else was hushed. Guests and servants held their breath in wonder. Or perhaps in fear that the earth would burst open once more and swallow the whole palace.

The earth held firm. I don't know how long we continued. We were under a spell. So were all who looked on, even Minos. He made no move to stop or to separate us.

Once, when the musicians paused, we spoke. "Theseus, look down," I said. "If only you could learn each line and angle, twist and turn of this mosaic floor by heart!" And I told him its secret as I had heard it from Daedalus's lips: "It is the Labyrinth made small." I told him how near death inside the Labyrinth I myself had come. I said, "Theseus, if you die tomorrow, I, too, will die, of grief."

"No, my Ariadne. We both will live." Theseus kissed the band that ringed my brow and said with blithe assurance, "You will come away with me, to be my wife and Athens' queen. But first you must help me. Will you?"

Chapter 6

WHEN THE FEAST ENDED, long past midnight, I went to Daedalus. He kept late hours. Often he worked on his inventions all night long.

I found him hunched over his worktable, peering through a magic glass. When he turned around to me, he saw at once that I was changed. "What has happened to you, little dove? Come, sit down. Tell me."

I told him everything and begged him, "Help me to help Theseus! Help us both!"

Whatever I had asked of him, starting when I was very small, he had never denied me. Now, to my vast disappointment, he wrinkled his high forehead, behind which I'd always thought lay all the wisdom of the world. And he said, "Don't put your trust in an Athenian."

"Daedalus, please, don't joke with me, not now! You yourself are Athenian."

"Yes, that is precisely why—"

"I know, I know," I cut him short, "you did some wrong, you had to flee, a long, long time ago when you were young. There's no time to talk about that now. In less than three hours it will be dawn. Do you hear the roaring?"

"Yes. Poor Minotaur. It's always like this at tribute time. His keepers starve him nearly to death, to make him all the hungrier for—"

"Theseus, he's going first! But he will not fall victim and be devoured. No! He is as strong as Heracles. Besides, the gods protect him. He will triumph."

"By slaying your mother's son?" asked my teacher quietly.

"Yes. Oh Daedalus, don't think that does not trouble me. It's true, Theseus will have to kill my mother's son. But, as you yourself have often said, they raised this son of my mother's to be a monster, and only to kill and kill."

Daedalus looked deep in thought. "If the gods will protect Theseus, as you say, what help does he need of you or me?"

"*You* know. After he has done what he intends, he must find his way out of the Labyrinth. You are its maker. You know its twists and turns as well as you know the lines and branchings of the palm of your own hand. Only you can help him. Please. It's a small thing I ask."

"No, there you are wrong, my dear. You ask an enormous thing of me. If I help you to help Theseus, you will flee with him. I will never see you again." Daedalus, for as long as I had known him, had never showed emotion. Now he did not even try to hide his sadness. His head sank down upon his chest. His eyes filled with tears. He said, "I will miss you, dearest dove, till the end of my days, as bitterly and sorely as I would miss my own child Icarus."

"Thank you for that." I was touched. I laid my cheek against his. "But wouldn't you miss me even more if I died? Which I will, instantly, if Theseus dies tomorrow, for he is my destiny."

"Are you quite certain, Ariadne?" Daedalus pushed the magic glass toward me. It had the power to turn tiny specks that you could

31

not normally see into quite large objects. "Close one eye. With the other eye, look through the lens."

I looked, and saw two metal parts for some mechanical toy that he was making. The edges of the two parts were jagged as serpents' teeth.

He said, "I tried very hard to fit those two parts together. I used all my skill and my best instruments. But I could not do it. Their ends—or, you might say, their destinies—oppose each other, will not mesh."

"But Daedalus, we are not made of metal, Theseus and I."

"You, for one, are not. There is tenderness and kindness in you. What Theseus is made of is a question. In part, at least, he's made of stern, unyielding stuff, or he had better be, for his destiny is to make Athens a great power. Many enemies will oppose him, and he will have to vanquish them. But your destiny, Ariadne, is here. All Crete looks to you to bring relief from your father's harsh reign."

"And so I shall, someday, with Theseus. But even more important, he and I must be together, be as one. Aphrodite wishes it." I told Daedalus how the goddess had caused apple blossom petals to shower down on me.

"Aphrodite can be capricious," said Daedalus. "Your duty is to Mother Dia of the Earth. Hers is the greater power."

"Daedalus, stop preaching to me! I counted on you, and you are failing me. How can you not understand? Don't you remember what love is like? Did you never give your heart away?"

"Take back your heart," he warned me.

"I can't! I could sooner rip it from my body!"

Daedalus sighed, closed his eyes. "I have heard those very words spoken before."

"Spoken by whom?" A shiver went through me. I knew what he would answer.

"By your mother, Pasiphae."

"And you helped her," I said, weeping. "So now I beg you, help her daughter, too."

"It is true, I helped your mother come together with her beloved. And we know the outcome all too well."

"But hers was a beast. *My* beloved is godlike and great."

"Those were your mother's words, exactly. And I could not refuse her."

I laid my head in Daedalus's lap. I said, "Don't refuse me."

He stroked my hair. "All right, I will help you. But first there is a place where we must go."

Yes, I knew.

We set out at once for the pasture, an hour's walk away, where my mother first caught sight of the godlike white bull. In the middle, surrounded by young cypress trees, was my mother's tomb.

Daedalus knelt at the foot of it. I bowed down. Daedalus had told me that silence is louder than speech when calling to the dead. Therefore, without speaking, we called upon my mother's shade and asked forgiveness for what would happen to her son if Theseus prevailed.

A softness came into the air. The moon spread a shimmer over the pasture. I felt released from the terrible fear that had been gnawing at me. An ease came over me.

Suddenly Daedalus broke the silence. "What wedding clothes?" he asked.

I was taken aback. "What do you mean?"

"Child, you spoke of wedding clothes just now. Were you not aware?"

I shook my head.

"Doubtless the shade of your dear mother spoke the words through your lips," said Daedalus.

Just then a rooster crowed. The blackness at the edge of the sky was starting to fade to gray.

Daedalus and I touched our foreheads to the tomb and hurried back to the palace, to his workroom.

He rummaged through a cabinet, took out a gleaming object, placed it in my hands. It was a spool of golden thread.

"This thread is strong. No power on earth can break it. Listen to me carefully. I will tell you how to use it."

When he had finished instructing me, he kissed me on the forehead. "I wish you greater fulfillment than even you have dreamed. Farewell, my precious dove."

Chapter 7

THE EDGE OF THE SKY WAS STREAKED WITH LIGHT. By the time I got back to my bedchamber, it was nearly dawn. In less than an hour, Theseus would be thrust into the Labyrinth.

I had no time for farewells to this room in which I'd never sleep again, nor to all the treasures of my childhood. Quickly I dashed water on my face, brushed the tangles from my hair. Quietly, so as not to waken my women, I opened my wardrobe. When my fingers touched my mother's wedding gown and mantle, I wept as on the day when she was laid into her tomb.

I was only five years old then, too young to attend the burial.

I'd hidden in her bedchamber. When her women came in to fold away her clothing, I'd clutched onto this gown, kissed each lily on its border, hidden my face in its soft linen folds. I'd pulled the mantle around me tight, begging the women, "Don't put these away." So they had let me keep the gown and mantle in my wardrobe where I could touch them, hide in them and weep whenever I had need.

Now I took them out. I laid my cheek against the lily-embroidered border of the gown. And my fears diminished. When I put on the gown, I felt as though my mother's shade were near me, assuring me that what I was about to do was right. When I put the mantle on, confidence arose in me that I would find in myself all the bravery and endurance my new life would require.

I strung the magic key onto the braided belt with which the gown was gathered below my bosom. And I took the golden spool.

But I could not leave without reaching up to touch the tawny cheeks of my lion painted on the wall above my bed. I gazed into his green-golden eyes, which had looked on me for all my years, and prepared to feel sharp pangs of parting grief. Instead, to my surprise, I felt a fierce, joyous certainty—I knew not from where it came—that he, companion of my dreams, and I would not be parted forever.

Then I hurried out.

The staircase and corridors were all but deserted. The few tradespeople and servants I encountered at this early hour were awed by my ceremonial clothing and paid me deep obeisance.

When I reached the antechamber to the Labyrinth, Theseus was already there. Five of the Minotaur's keepers, wearing crimson kilts in honor of the bloody day, surrounded him and searched him.

Theseus allowed it. "You won't find any weapon," he said, holding up his fists. "These fists"—he punched the air with mighty blows—"are all the weapons I will need."

The keepers laughed. "Your fists will not defend you from our Minotaur," said one.

"The Minotaur's jaws will chop clean as a butcher's knife," said another.

"You will not—" started a third, but the words froze on his lips. He fell to his knees, terror-stricken when he saw me standing there dressed in my mother's clothes. "Your M-m-majesty, Qu-qu-queen P-P-Pasiphae," he stammered, "why have you come back from the dead?"

The other keepers also knelt down.

I moved my hand over their helmets, as though blessing them. Theseus looked on, amused.

"Blessed shade of our queen, do not harm us," they begged. "What would you have us do? Command us, and we will obey."

"Release the victim to my care," I commanded in my most queenly voice.

But just then the chief keeper arrived, the same one who, so many years ago, had saved me from the Minotaur and betrayed me to my father. He kicked the others on their backsides. "Why are you groveling?"

They stammered and pointed at me.

He read their thoughts and laughed at them. "The dead stay dead. This lady is the princess Ariadne. On your feet, you superstitious fools, there's work to do. The Minotaur is famished. If we don't send him his breakfast soon, he'll come charging out and help himself to one of us. Athenian, prepare to die." He clasped Theseus by the shoulder and marched him toward the door.

I stepped in front of them, making my body a barrier.

With all the majesty I had in me I ordered the chief keeper, "Kneel down!"

He obeyed.

I stood before him straight as a statue, arms raised in the posture that Mother Dia's chief priestess had taught me. My hands described the writhing spirals that the Goddess's sacred temple snakes make, the meaning of which only priestesses can know. "Chief keeper, hear me: I shall not prevent you from carrying out your duty. But know that I, too, have a duty. The Goddess commands—" Here I faltered and almost lost my courage. But a glance from Theseus spurred me on. "The Goddess commands that you not interfere with my duty. You may rise."

All Cretans know that to go against the mighty Goddess's will

38

could cause one's organs to shrivel up, bring on a deadly pox, all manner of ills.

The keeper rose up from kneeling and stood with his head bowed.

I unwound a length of golden thread. Then I took Theseus's hand, tied the end of the thread around his left middle finger, knotted the thread securely, and said, "I will hold the spool however long I must. The thread will guide you back to me. No force on earth can cause it to break."

The light of understanding came into his eyes. He embraced me. Then he strode forward, into the Labyrinth.

I stood and listened to his footfalls growing faint. I paid out more and more golden thread as he advanced farther and farther away. Soon I could no longer hear his steps. But the way the spool moved in the palms of my hands spoke to me clearly, as though in a new language, telling me that Theseus kept a steady pace and that his spirit was undaunted.

I went up to the door. The keepers gave me room and did not interfere. I had to stand on tiptoe to reach the double ax affixed to it. This ax was sacred to the Goddess. I touched my forehead and my lips to each blade. And I implored her, "Mother Dia, help him. Help us both."

My hands became attuned to every slight movement of the spool, enabling me to share in Theseus's emotions almost as though I were by his side as he progressed toward the center of the Labyrinth in which the Minotaur, scenting flesh, roared and roared.

This continued for many hours.

Suddenly the spool gave a violent twitch. So did my heart. I could almost see the cruel horns, the bloodshot eyes, the foaming muzzle as the Minotaur came charging. I could feel in my sinews that the battle had begun, and Theseus's life lay in the balance.

The keepers sat cross-legged on the floor, oblivious. They were

throwing dice, calling out numbers, shouting with glee when they won. Meanwhile my heart thumped and thudded as the spool contorted in my hands.

Then came one loud roar so full of bloodthirst and triumph that even the keepers interrupted their game. An icy dread crept over me. I trembled so hard, I had to grip the spool with all my might for fear that it might fall.

"Mother Dia, hear me now!" I sank to my knees once more and begged her forgiveness for pretending to be here by her will.

She answered me. I know not if I fainted, as seers do, or went into a trance. I heard her words distinctly, coming through the roaring:

"Daughter, all life that springs from Earth is sacred. It is my most ancient will that animals not be slaughtered on my altars. The sacrifice of animal blood offends me. The wanton spilling of human blood in this Labyrinth year upon year offends me even more."

It was while I listened to these words that the roaring ceased. Now the only sound was the rattling of the dice. All else was deadly still. In my mind's eye I saw the Minotaur triumphant, starting his bloody feast. "Mother Dia," I cried out, "Great Mother of the Earth, let this not be!"

A long drawn-out moaning issued from the Labyrinth, anguished and low. All the while it lasted, my heart did not beat, my blood stood still in my veins. When it ceased, the spool gave a leap in my hands. And I knew that the Minotaur was dead.

Now the thread grew slack, made loops on the floor. I wound them up and kissed the spool for giving me this proof that Theseus was alive and moving. "Golden thread, guide him back to me," I whispered, and began the long vigil of winding up, paying out again, and winding, winding up again and again, as Theseus made his way through the countless passages.

At long last I heard his footsteps. The keepers were arguing heatedly over who had won the last throw and did not look up as I slipped through the door.

I ran through the first passageway. Then I saw him, ashen, drenched in sweat, dragging himself along. "I throttled him," he whispered hoarsely. "He was your kin. Do not think ill of me."

I could think no other thought than taking Theseus in my arms. This I did, and felt his strength returning—just in time.

Two keepers came running toward us. Faster than arrows from Apollo's bow, Theseus's fists shot out and he dealt them such blows, to the chin, to the ears, between the eyes, they fell backward insensible.

Chapter 8

THE KEEPERS IN THE ANTECHAMBER met with just such blows and soon lay unconscious on the floor.

Theseus removed the chief keeper's kilt and helmet. "Be so kind as to lend me these. In return, here is my tunic." He took it off, laid it over the keeper. "There, now you won't be cold." He put on the keeper's kilt and helmet.

Together we carried the keepers into the Labyrinth, laid them down beside the other two, hurried out, locked the three stout iron locks behind us.

Then, walking at a stately pace, with dignified expressions on our faces, we made our way through the palace corridors. Passersby bowed down to us, stepped aside respectfully to let the royal princess and the Minotaur's chief keeper pass.

We went up the central staircase and out by the gate at which litter bearers congregated.

I asked a team of four stout-looking fellows to take us to the prison house down by the harbor.

They were startled, and protested that their litter was not fit for royalty.

"No matter," I said. "We bear a message of great importance from my father to the warden. The faster you bring us there, the more generously will my father reward you."

We got in. The road to the harbor sloped downward, so the bearers could run all the way.

The prison in which the young Athenians were shut was a grim, unornamented building of gray stone.

The guard at the door bowed to me respectfully, but was suspicious of Theseus and asked him to identify himself.

"Can't you tell by this kilt and helmet that I am chief keeper of the Minotaur?"

"Not so," said the guard. "My friend Eratos holds that post."

"No longer," said Theseus with perfect composure. "Your friend Eratos is a coward. Minos himself dismissed him and appointed me to take his place. The princess is my witness. Go, fellow. We have no time for chatter. Tell your warden we must see him at once."

The guard went to fetch him.

The warden came. A corpulent man with jowls and a great belly, he was none too pleased at having had to interrupt his noonday meal. "Aegleia, bring my food!" he shouted.

A young Athenian woman of great beauty came in, carrying a tray. I remembered her at once. She was the one who had preceded Theseus off the tribute ship.

She saw through Theseus's disguise. Her mouth fell open. She nearly dropped the tray and would have cried out his name. But he said, "Theseus is dead, slain by the Minotaur." He turned to the warden and demanded, "By whose authority do you use this prisoner to serve your personal needs?"

"I didn't—I only—" The warden was much embarrassed.

"You shall answer for it," Theseus said with cool authority. "We are here by the king's command. He bids you assemble the young

Athenians as quickly as possible. We will conduct them to the palace, where they are to view their leader's earthly remains."

The warden frowned. "This has not been the custom."

"Nor has it been the custom for a prince of Athens to fall prey to the Minotaur," said I.

Begging my pardon, the warden asked if we brought written orders from the king.

Theseus rebuked him. "Have you no respect for royal persons? Is not the princess's presence here proof enough for you? Look to your position, warden. The work is easy, the pay is good, but you won't enjoy it for much longer when the king hears of your discourtesy to us."

The warden begged our pardon. He struck a gong, whereupon two prison guards let in the twelve Athenians.

Theseus kept his visor down lest any recognize him.

"My guards will take them to the palace," said the warden, and offered us the use of his own private litter and bearers.

"No. We ourselves will take them," said Theseus. "Guards, loosen their shackles."

When this was done, we led them out the door and around to the rear of the prison. In the shelter of a wall I took my key, unlocked their shackles, and made them swear on their honor as Athenians not to utter cries or shouts of joy.

Theseus took off his helmet.

All but one were true to their oaths. They swarmed around him silently, shedding tears of gladness.

Only Aegleia shouted, "I knew you would come!" and threw her arms around him.

"Hush, Aegleia."

Her name on his lips, the long moment that passed before he removed her arms from around him, brought a sharp sensation, like a serpent's sting, to my bosom. I banished the feeling. I had no time for it now.

"Shipmates, run for the harbor," Theseus commanded. They took off like a flock of birds.

In my mother's garments I could not keep pace. Theseus walked by my side.

When we reached the dock, the others had stripped and dived in. Their red tunics floated like giant flowers on the water.

"I can't swim in these clothes," I said. "And I must not leave them behind."

"You need not." Theseus lowered himself into the water. He made summoning motions with his arms, as I had seen him do that other time, and prayed to Poseidon, "Lend my shipmates strength!"

Then he so positioned them that they formed a human bridge from the dock to the SEA DOVE.

"Come, Ariadne, walk across. The bridge is strong. It will hold."

He took my hand as I stepped off the dock. I willed my body to be light.

The young Athenians bore my weight, showing no signs of strain. Theseus swam alongside.

By then the sun stood high in the sky. It was the time most people spend indoors at their noon meal or resting. Once I looked back and saw a dock worker staring, struck dumb with wonder. No doubt he took me for the shade of my dead mother. How else explain the mystery of a woman walking on water?

Aegleia was the last link of the bridge. Stepping on to her body, I wondered, was there hatred in her extraordinary violet-blue eyes? Or did they merely mirror my own feelings? At any rate, her gaze unnerved me, and I nearly lost my balance as I reached for the ship's ladder and started to climb up.

The others followed—all but Theseus.

"Helmsman, hand me down an oar," he called, "a stout one,

edged with iron. Then weigh anchor, be off, don't wait for me!"

Theseus straddled the oar and, rowing powerfully with his arms, propelled himself toward my father's fleet lying at anchor in the harbor.

When he came close to the flagship, he lifted the oar, thrust it forward with all his strength. Doubtless Poseidon lent *his* strength, too. For the gash the oar made in the flagship's side was huge.

I stood and watched from the stern. Meanwhile a stiff southerly wind had arisen. It churned up white-crested waves and drove the S E A D O V E forward, leaving Theseus far behind.

Poseidon must have lent him a swift-footed horse. For, quicker than humanly possible, Theseus came riding over the waves and climbed aboard.

"I had to stave in your father's ship to prevent his fleet from catching up with us and wresting you from me." And again he said, "Do not think ill of me."

"I will never think ill of you," I breathed, so glad was I to have him near me. Spent with exhaustion and emotion, I entered into his embrace.

Chapter 9

BEHIND MY EYELIDS ALL WAS DARK. My body felt in motion, as though rocked by waves, lulled by their rhythmic swelling and receding. My head was pillowed softly—on Theseus's chest, I thought. Warmth enveloped me.

I tried to hear his breathing, but could not. I only heard the waves. "How quietly he sleeps," I thought.

"Theseus," I whispered softly, careful not to disturb the other sleepers on board. I turned, reached out, reached all around, touched only emptiness.

The warmth came from my mother's mantle covering me. The softness under my head was her gown. It had been carefully folded to serve as a pillow.

I wore only a light, short undergarment. I felt for the golden band. It still encircled my head.

When I tried to stand up, I struck my head against a rough, curving surface. It was the roof of a dark cave. I followed a shaft of light on the ground and groped my way to the opening.

Bright daylight met my eyes. The sun stood high in a cloudless sky. All around me lay the sea, dark blue with white crested wavelets. On and in between them floated gulls and other sea-birds.

The cave I had slept in was a short distance up a rocky slope. Below it were outcroppings of boulders, perhaps of marble, some rose-pink, others of an astonishing whiteness. Waves lapped against the lowest ones, leaving them clothed in collars of foam.

I climbed down to the water's edge.

In contrast to the dazzling daylight, darkness shrouded my mind. "Don't think about what has happened to you," some power commanded me, "or the darkness will engulf you wholly." I sat down on a rock and banished all thoughts, tried to make my mind as blank as a wax tablet belonging to a child who does not know how to write and has no stylus with which to make marks.

I looked out over the endless expanse of sea. I made believe that time could move backward, that it was the morning of the feast again, that just beyond the great boulders behind me stood the shrine of Aphrodite, goddess-champion of Theseus's journey. I shut my eyes and summoned back the moment when Theseus had come leaping down the hillside to me.

But time is deaf to human wishes. Moments don't return. Nor do thoughts stay banished. I thought of Aphrodite. I prayed to her, "Goddess by whose will Theseus and I are one, and who showered apple blossoms on me, send me another sign."

But even as I prayed, Daedalus's words came back to me: "Aphrodite can be capricious."

Memory, too, can be capricious. Mine chose that moment to bring a picture to the fore that Daedalus had showed me once as part of a lesson. It was of a large, odd-looking bird that lived in Africa, called the ostrich. "The ostrich is a stupid bird. When he is in danger, he prefers not to know about it. So he buries his head in the sand," Daedalus had said. "Ostrich!" I could hear him call me as plainly as if he were sitting beside me.

49

What place was this? How had I come here? For what purpose? By whose will?

I tried to clear away the fog that enveloped my brain. I recalled being on the ship: Theseus leading me to a sheltered place below the half-deck; the boatswain calling to the crew, "Take down the black sail, hoist the white." For Theseus's father had asked that a white sail be the sign that Theseus still lived and was returning in triumph.

"The sail can wait," Theseus had shouted back. "Minos has many ships beside the one I disabled. They will pursue us. Let us gain all the headway we can." He took the boatswain's drum and beat on it, urging the oarsmen to row with all their might.

The SEA DOVE all but flew, heading north-northwest.

When we could not see the harbor anymore, Theseus gave orders to change course. "Minos will assume that we make straight for Athens. Therefore let us sail north-northeastward, toward—"

He named a destination I could not remember. He had been holding a flask to my lips. I was parched. All I recalled was a soothing, cool liquid pouring into my mouth. It tasted of exotic spices and oblivion.

Doubtless there was poppy in it. Else I would not have slept so long and deeply, and would certainly have wakened when I was taken from the ship and brought onto this island.

North-northeast of Knossos are Thera, Naxos, Samos, countless islands. Which one was this? Who lived here besides me? What lay beyond where I could see?

I stood up. I picked my way along the rocks, trying to avoid the prickly, spiny mollusks that clung to them.

Where the rocks ended lay a stretch of whitest beach. The sand blazed in the sun, causing the air to shimmer. Some distance away, a flock of gulls tore with their beaks at clumps of sea grass full of the remains of shrimp and crabs.

When I came near them they set up a shrieking. It sounded like malicious laughter, and would have been exactly that, if gulls were mean of spirit and could read. For written in large letters in the sand were these words:

"The gods are jealous of our love. Do not think ill of me. Theseus."

I read it over and over. I spoke it aloud. But the words were merely sounds. I could not make sense of them. They held no meaning. Nor did this sand, this beach. Nor did my life. It was as though my heart, my brain, and all the other places in my body that had once been open to meanings and feelings, had frozen solid, turned to ice.

Yet the noonday sun blazed hotly down on me.

Without thinking what I was doing, I took off my shift and walked into the sea. It was shallow. I had to walk quite far before it reached my knees.

A few paces farther, the ground dropped away abruptly. Good. To drop away abruptly myself was what I wanted. Then I would be spared the pain of meanings.

I told my feet, my legs, my arms, my hands, "Be still. Do nothing at all."

But they obeyed a different voice that once had told them, "Kick, flutter, push the water away"—Cleia's voice from long ago when, at a secret beach we'd found, she'd taught me how to swim.

I swam far out. The sea was dark, yet clear. I could see far down into its depths, where bright-colored fish wove in and out among swaying grasses. When I turned onto my back and floated on the waves, I saw the dance of black swifts and swallows and of white-winged terns and gulls swooping, circling in the bright blue air.

It was splendid. I could not help but revel in it.

Afterwards I put off returning to the dark cave and went exploring.

The ground above the cave rose steeply through woods of oaks, pines, almond trees, and cypresses.

The higher I went, the faster I climbed, eager to reach an open place from which to look out. Hope had taken root in me, a foolish hope, I knew.

When I had climbed almost to the top, I finally came to a clearing that offered a view. I stood beside a cypress tree and scanned the long, wide, curving horizon where the sea and sky seemed to meld into each other. I willed a speck to come into view. I strained with every nerve and sinew to make it happen. "Appear!" I implored. "Draw near, take on the form of a ship. One with a black sail, and a prow in the shape of a dove's beak—"

What pitiful creatures humans are! What reasons have gods or goddesses ever to be jealous of us? They can take a mote of dust and shape it into any form they want. They can make happen whatever they wish. They never need yearn, as do the likes of us. "Us"—the word pierced me like a dagger. That "us" of which I had been one half was no more, was ripped apart. Now there was just aloneness.

Those were my thoughts. I had done right, trying to banish them.

When I could no longer endure the glare of the sun upon the endless, empty sea, I left that place and went down the slope. My stomach cramped with hunger. My lips and mouth were cracked and dry from thirst. All along the way grew dandelion greens, good mushrooms, red, ripe berries. I did not pick a one. I came to a clear, frothing spring, but I did not drink from it.

Behind the cave flowed a brook. There I stooped and washed myself. I wanted to be clean for Death's messenger. I hoped he would come soon.

It was still not night. No matter, my cave was dark. I lay down, covered myself with my mother's mantle, closed my eyes.

Sleep would not come. In the stillness, I heard the sea gulls laughing at me, heard Theseus's message, over and over: "The gods are jealous of our love. Do not think ill of me."

My feelings broke free of their icy prison and seethed and roiled in me. The gods, jealous? Well, perhaps. But not as jealous as I! I recalled Aegleia gazing up at me. Was it for her that Theseus left me here? I wished Aegleia dead. I wished all women dead that he would ever love. When had he stopped loving me? Or had he never loved me, but merely pretended, in order to gain my help? Oh yes, I *did* think ill of him. Bitter, ugly ill.

"Us, us, us!" The word resounded in my head, mocked me more cruelly than the sea gulls had done with their laughter. I could not get free of "us." Here I was, discarded on this godforsaken island, utterly alone, yet still I felt a part of Theseus.

"Hermes, messenger of death, come soon," I begged. "Come before these ugly, bitter thoughts cause bats' wings to grow from my shoulders, and I turn into some monstrous, evil creature of fury and revenge."

Chapter 10

NEXT DAWN FOUND ME AT THE BROOK, scooping up water with both hands, gulping it down. As soon as I slaked my thirst, I picked all the berries, mushrooms, lettuce, wild fennel, and wild celery I saw and stuffed them in my mouth.

Meanwhile a thousand birds sang in the trees all around. It sounded like a hymn of thanks to the sun for rising once again. And I wondered, did any birds *not* join in? Birds who sorrowed for lost loves? Birds who longed to die? I pictured them grieving inside their nests, not venturing forth to sip water or hunt for worms or grubs or flies.

If such birds existed, they were more staunch than I, gorging myself, swallowing down food as fast as I could, and still not getting enough.

Looking for more berries, I entered into a lush, dense thicket. There I saw a kind I'd never seen before—deep, plump, smooth, dark blue berries hanging down in clusters from a tall green vine.

"Don't eat berries unless you know what they are," my old nurse

used to warn me and tell grizzly stories of people who had done so and been poisoned to death.

Well, if these would poison me, so much the better. I reached up, grasped one between my thumb and forefinger, tried to pluck it. But the cluster shook itself free and disappeared from view as though with a will of its own.

As I stood on tiptoes, reaching into the thicket to retrieve it, something touched my arm. It wasn't leaves or thorns, no, for it had fur, or hair, on it—and fingers. Then I heard a sound, a kind of bleating, chuckling laughter.

Or was I imagining it all, as wanderers do who are lost in a desert, when their minds are addled and cause them to see water shimmering before them where all is deadly dry? Had grief and aloneness addled *my* mind? Were the luscious-looking berries, the touch to my skin, and the laughter mere illusions?

Was I going mad? That thought alarmed me more than dying.

"Is anyone there?" I shouted.

Yes—someone grasped me by the waist.

"Oh, let it be Hermes!" I said aloud.

This caused a burst of loud laughter. A strange creature, distinctly male, came forth from the undergrowth. He had hoofs for feet. His arms and legs were covered with fur-like, wavy white and brownish hair. The hair on his head was thick and curly, and grew down low over his forehead almost to his eyes, which were yellow, like a goat's. His nose, mouth, cheeks, and chin were those of a boy. His body was that of a man in his prime. Yet something about him seemed ancient.

"You took me for Hermes, that somber god? That leader of souls to death's kingdom? Why ever in the lush, green world would you pray for *him* to come to you?"

"I long for death," I answered.

"Dear me. You are so young. How can that be?" He reached

57

behind him into a thicket, brought out the cluster of berries. "Have some. You'll find them sweeter than dying. Go on."

"First tell me, what place is this? And who and what are you?"

"This is the island of Naxos. I am a satyr. My name is Penthilus, 'Assuager of Grief.' " He bowed low from the waist, all the while grinning broadly. "Do, please, taste these berries." He plucked a perfect one and put it to my lips.

I had to taste it. It was of a sweet, rich tartness unlike anything that ever crossed my lips before.

"Now you must tell me who you are and why you are so sad," said Penthilus.

"Ariadne—" The name sounded broken, a shard of something no longer in life. I hung my head. "No, I am not who I was."

"You are not? How can that be? I have always been who I am. Well, perhaps not always. But for longer than these trees and bushes have been here. Tell me, how is it possible not to be who you were?" His yellow eyes regarded me with insistent wonder.

"I gave up my home," I tried to explain. "I left everything behind, all for the sake of another. I put my past and future in the hands of that other. I poured my whole self into his being. Now he is gone. I have lost him and, along with him, my own entire self."

Penthilus wrinkled his low brow as though deep in thought. "Let me try to understand. Was this other of whom you speak your first love?"

"You don't, you cannot understand!" I cried. "Yes, first, and also last. What *I* experienced can happen only once."

He put on a sad look. But laughter gleamed in his eyes.

"You are ill-named," I accused him. "You are no 'Assuager of Grief,' but a coarse, heartless creature. It's useless explaining my-self to the likes of you." I turned my back on him and fled to my cave.

Later, as I lay awake, thoughts of the dark blue berries came to me uninvited and interrupted my grief. I longed to burst those berries' skin, taste their tart, sweet juice. And I thought, as I lay suspended between wakefulness and dreaming, "Surely the gods on Olympus feast on such berries along with their nectar and ambrosia."

Chapter 11

NEXT MORNING I HEARD FLUTING SOUNDS—music that blended with the birds' and chased away my mournful dreams.

I hurried outside. The piper was gone but had left me a cluster of the dark blue berries on a bed of green vine leaves.

The following morning, I found a basket of wild mushrooms and greens.

The morning after that, there were two gifts.

One was a reed pipe. I tried to play it. But out came such sour sounds, such squawks and squeaks, I laughed out loud and was much astonished, for I thought I had forgotten how.

The second gift was a wreath of daisies, poppies, and clover blossoms just like wreaths that Cleia used to weave for me. But this one had leaves of the vine intertwined with the flowers and was more beautiful.

I put it on. And a strange thing happened: The golden band I had been wearing all this time pressed hard against my temples, as though protesting. As though the flower wreath were an offense to it.

I took off the wreath. I hung it on a stone that jutted out from the wall. It looked beautiful there and seemed to make the whole cave less dank and dark.

Late that day, in my wanderings, I saw smoke rising in the distance. I smelled firewood and roasting meat. My stomach, clenching with hunger, commanded my feet to run. Soon I came to a meadow with a brook running through it. Leaning against an oak-tree trunk sat the satyr Penthilus, tending the fire, giving the spit a turn.

He was glad to see me. "You came just in time," he said. "I snared a fine fat rabbit. It's almost ready. Will you do me the honor of sharing my feast?"

My stomach commanded me to answer "Yes."

"Good. I'm glad to have your company." He cast down his eyes as though suddenly shy. "And you needn't worry. We satyrs have a reputation for, well, being playful—'lewd, wanton,' humans say. But we are different now. In this time of loss, we lack the heart for it. You are quite safe with me."

He turned the spit to roast the meat evenly. He rubbed it with coriander, thyme, and laurel leaves, and basted it with its own juices that he had collected in a bowl carved out of wood.

Then he picked some dock weed leaves, folded them deftly, knotting the stems together. "Here is a good green plate for you." He tested the meat. Its juices ran clear. "It's done." He cut me a slice.

It was more delicious than any meat served on silver platters in my father's palace. I ate slowly, allowing time for my stomach to unclench.

I asked him, "Why is this a time of loss for you?"

He sighed. "I wish I could tell you, but I cannot."

"I wish you could, too." I thanked him for the feast and for his kind gifts to me.

"But did you not like the flower wreath?" he asked.

"Yes, very much—"

"Then why are you not wearing it?"

"Oh, Penthilus, I wanted to. But I could not, on account of this band I must wear—"

"Was it a gift from the 'other' of whom you spoke so sadly?" This question made my eyes overflow. He did not press me for an answer but spoke of other things: How he had snared the rabbit. Where he had found the reed from which he had carved the pipe for me. And he asked, "Do you like it?"

"Yes, very much, though I cannot play it very well."

"That is easily remedied. I have my pipe right here." He picked it up from where it lay and showed me with which fingers to cover up the different holes and how to draw breath from deep within me to bring forth rounded, singing tones.

Then we ate more meat until we were full.

"Now I have a great thirst," said Penthilus and drank from the brook. "Ah, water is good. But wine is better."

"What is 'wine?'" I asked.

"I wish I had some to give you. But we pledged to forego it. Perhaps forever. But I'll tell you what I'll do: I'll show you how it's made. Watch."

He stood up. He rounded his back, stooped down, danced to the left, then to the right, snapping his fingers, grasping, ungrasping the air. Then he jumped in place, bringing his hoofs down as though to crush the ground.

"What dance is that?" I asked.

"It is the *Epilenios,* dance of gathering grapes—"

"What are grapes?" I interrupted.

"The berries that you like so well. They are what wine is made of. First we pluck them, like so." He repeated the quick steps and finger motions. "Then we drop them into vats. Then we press out their sweet juices, like so." He jumped and stamped, all the while singing aloud.

Though neither delicate nor graceful, this dance had a great power. It pulled me in. Before I knew it I, too, stooped, stepped to the left, to the right, snapped my fingers, grasped, let go, jumped, and stamped my feet hard, hard, as though I were truly stamping on grapes, pressing out their juices. Yet the heavier I trod, the lighter I felt, as though my feet were trampling on my grief, stamping its weight into the ground. And the louder I sang along with Penthilus, the lighter grew the load around my heart.

We danced and sang ourselves breathless and collapsed laughing onto the grass.

Suddenly his eyes grew wide. He asked in a hushed voice, "Are you a princess?"

"Why do you want to know?"

"Never mind. Are you? Tell me."

I answered, "Yes."

Sweat broke out on his forehead. Fires flickered in his eyes.

"A princess dancing the *Epilenios*—" he said in a high, sharp voice, as though someone else, a woman, were speaking through him. Then his eyes went dull and glassy. His head sank onto his chest. He slumped sideways onto the ground and lay there shivering.

I touched him on the shoulder. He felt ice-cold.

Quickly I gathered all the dock weed leaves and other thick, broad leaves that I could find and covered him with them.

I sat beside him, holding his forehead. His cheeks were white. His eyes were open, but not seeing. His breath came in rasps and gasps. He was in a faint.

In a while it passed. Soon color returned to his face. He felt warmer to the touch. His eyes closed of their own accord.

So did my eyes for a few moments. And I dreamed of a ship sailing toward this island.

But it was more than a dream. It did not fade; it still possessed me, even when I opened my eyes. "It's Theseus," I thought. "He is returning. He was only testing me." I felt to blame for having eaten

heartily, for having danced with abandon—as though it was *I* who had broken faith with *him*.

Penthilus's breath came evenly, interspersed with snores. I left him to his peaceful sleep and clambered up the steep slope to find another place from which to look out over the sea.

A breeze was blowing—filling the sails of the S E A D O V E, I was certain.

But when I came to a place with an open view, no ship was in sight.

My dream receded. I don't know how long I stood there feeling empty as the sea. Finally Penthilus came climbing up and looked out, scanned the horizon just as I had done, and said, "I'm looking for a ship—"

"Shame on you, Penthilus. You make fun of me."

"Not so, Princess. A ship will come, I promise you."

We watched together. No sail appeared. Though Penthilus stood beside me, I felt more alone than in all my days on this island.

"Please don't be sad," he said.

"Why should I not be sad, abandoned on this godforsaken island?"

"Godforsaken this island has been, but shall not be for long. You yourself have shown me this," said Penthilus.

"What do you mean? You make no sense," I said.

"Nor did the oracle make sense, or so we satyrs thought."

"What oracle do you speak of, Penthilus?"

"One in a grove not far from here, ringed about with laurel bushes. This island, you see, is a favorite place of the god whom satyrs follow."

"What god? What is his name?"

"I cannot tell you. But listen to me, Princess. One night we satyrs had much reveling and slept a drunken sleep. When we awoke we were bereft. The god was gone. We went to the oracle and asked its priestess what became of him. 'Pirates seized him,' she replied. 'They took him away, perhaps to sell for a slave.' "

"How could a god let that happen?" I asked. "Could he not get free?"

"He was still very young. He had not come into the fullness of his powers," said Penthilus. "We asked the priestess where the pirates took him, and if and when he would return. 'Ask me no more,' she replied and went into a sacred frenzy, mouthing words over and over. We cursed her, thinking it was babble."

"What babble? What words?" I asked.

" 'A princess dancing the *Epilenios*—' " said Penthilus and disappeared.

Utter exhaustion came over me then. My arms and legs grew heavy, as though made of lead. I lay down in the grass. "At last I am near death," I thought, my eyelids falling shut.

Chapter 12

THE RADIANCE OF A THOUSAND SUMMERS' SUNS lit up the world for me. If this was a dream, it felt more real than my whole life before. A lion leaped into view. *My* lion. The one who, in my bedchamber in the palace at Knossos, had gazed down on me from the wall above my bed. But he was changed. His green-golden eyes had turned darkly glowing from joy. I knew not what joy. But I knew for certain I was meant to share it.

I arose from out of my sleeping self lying there on the ground. And I began a dance for him. My feet felt light, my heart felt light. I knew my grief was over.

Into my dream came a ship. It had a single broad white sail and was slender and curved as a sliver of moon. I saw a figure clothed in purple standing motionless before the mast, as though bound to it.

Yes, and suddenly he burst the bonds and broke free.

In that moment the ship's mast sprouted leaves and became a vine. Great clusters of dark blue grapes hung from it. The figure that had sprung free crouched on the deck and became a lion, snarled, lashing out at other figures, sailors. Terrified, they jumped overboard, and in midair were changed into dolphins.

Now that the ship was lighter, it all but flew toward this island, Naxos.

In my dream—if a dream it was—I clambered sure-footed down the slope and heard a chorus swelling in song, as though all the trees of the woods, all the rocks and cliffs and pebbles and shells down at the shore had suddenly been granted voices and joined together with birds, with every living creature singing, "Ariadne, awake!"

And just as the ship's mast had changed into a fruitful vine, my dream was changed to waking.

Clothed in my mother's festive garments, I stood on the beach of Naxos, my arms open wide to the lion. With powerful strokes he swam ashore. He shook the water from him. He lifted a forepaw and stroked my face more tenderly than any human touch had ever done.

Yes, then it came to me who this lion was.

I clasped his paw. I held it to my breast. It changed, became a hand. The lion took on human form, the form of a man, very young. His long black hair hung down in curls. He was robed in purple. In his right hand he held an ivy-and-vine-wreathed staff with a pinecone at the tip. All that remained of his earlier form was a lion skin draped over his shoulder.

I stood before him trembling, waiting for him to speak.

He spoke my name, "Ariadne," thereby healing its brokenness, making it whole. "Do you know me?"

He made a motion with his hands. I knew what he was asking. I took the golden band off my head and placed it in his hands.

Then I knew the true source of the radiance. It was the light in this young god's eyes, disclosing himself to me.

"You who know me, hear my name: I am Dionysus, newly come

into my power. Accept me. I am the god of gladness and of life."

I fell to my knees. The knowledge suffused me that by doing so, I was not breaking my oath to Mother Dia—no, on the contrary, I was keeping it all the more.

He laid his hand on my head. Then he raised me up. "You serve the Goddess Mother Dia still," he said, reading what was in my heart. "It is by her will that I find you on this island I hold dear. My mother Semele was of the Earth. She served Mother Dia too. And so do I, most gratefully. For it is she who makes the vine grow. We will serve her together, you and I."

He gazed down at my golden band. "No earthly love is in vain," he said. "Even love that ends in pain and grief is precious as a stop along the way toward greater love." He swung his arm far back, as discus throwers do, and hurled the golden headband up into the air.

It rose higher than the island's summit. It soared into the blue. Finally I could no longer see it.

"You will see it when the sky grows dark," said Dionysus. "It will be a star. It will shine forever. And through all the ages to come, all the world will know of Ariadne's love for Theseus—"

"As a stop along the way to a greater love," I said, looking into his eyes. Their depths were as measureless as the height to which the golden band had soared. I went into his arms. The horses of Helios, and with them time itself, came to a halt.

When time resumed its course, Penthilus came bounding down the cliff, agile as a mountain goat. In one hand he carried two wreaths of vine leaves and grapes. In the other hand he held a flask. He placed one wreath on Dionysus's brow, the other wreath on mine.

"A princess danced the *Epilenios:* the soothsaying is fulfilled!" Penthilus was jubilant. "Mighty god, I brought the news to every satyr, nymph, and naiad on this island. They are coming from their hidden places. They will soon be here to greet you."

70

"And to take part in our wedding," said Dionysus. He took the flask from Penthilus and handed it to me. This time I knew what it was I drank: the juices of grapes made into wine that the satyrs had foresworn for as long as their god was absent. Then Dionysus drank, and then Penthilus, tears of gladness flowing down his cheeks.

As a god newly come into his power, Dionysus could make happen whatever he wished. But he saw fit to kiss the hem of my gown. And he asked, "Will you have me, Ariadne?"

"Yes, oh yes, I will." Immeasurable joy filled my being, a joy I knew would last me all my days on earth.

Epilogue

ARIADNE LIVED A GLORIOUS LIFE with her husband, the god Dionysus. They had many children together. They traveled the world over, teaching people the arts of cultivating grapes and making wine.

As for Theseus, various reasons have been proposed why he abandoned Ariadne on Naxos—that he did so at Aphrodite's, or Dionysus's, command; that he was fickle, in love with someone else; or that he feared that this princess of Crete was too mighty in her own right and would outshine him.

In any case, he returned to Athens. But he forgot to hoist the white sail as the signal to his father Aegeus that all was well. When Aegeus caught sight of the ship with its black sail drawing near, he thought that Theseus had been killed. Despairing, Aegeus threw himself from a high cliff to his death. This, according to some, was Theseus's punishment.

About the Author

DORIS ORGEL was born in Austria and graduated from Barnard College. She has worked as a translator and reviewer of children's books, as well as a children's book writer. Her books for Viking and Puffin include *The Devil in Vienna, My War with Mrs. Galloway, Whiskers Once and Always, Midnight Soup and a Witch's Hat, Starring Becky Suslow,* and *Nobodies and Somebodies.* She is currently a member of the Bank Street Writers' Group. She lives in New York City.

About the Illustrator

BARRY MOSER has been referred to as, "one of the most important [artists] working today" (*Publishers Weekly*). His work is represented in numerous collections, museums, and libraries throughout the world, and he has received many awards. Some of the books he has illustrated are *Alice's Adventures in Wonderland,* which won the American Book Award; and *Little Tricker the Squirrel Meets Big Double the Bear* by Ken Kesey, the 1992 IBBY Honor Book, and *Prayers from the Ark* by Carmen Bernos de Gasztold, translated by Rumer Godden (both Viking). Mr. Moser lives in western Massachusetts.

74